Goldilocks and the Three Bears

ıis Weber, C.E.O.
blications International, Ltd.
3 North Cicero Avenue
ıcolnwood, Illinois 60646

Manufactured in the U.S.A.

8   7   6   5   4   3   2   1

ISBN 1-56173-915-4

Cover illustration by Sam Thiewes

Book illustrations by Burgandy Nilles

Story adapted by Jane Jerrard

Publications International, Ltd.

There once was a family of three bears. There was a great big Papa Bear, a middle-size Mama Bear, and a wee little Baby Bear. The three bears lived in a cozy little house right in the middle of the forest.

The three bears always started each day in the very same way. First, they washed their faces and paws with sparkling fresh water and sweet-smelling soap. Then they made their beds and fluffed their feather pillows. And after they were dressed for the day, they went downstairs for a nice breakfast of delicious porridge.

One bright morning, Mama Bear cooked the porridge and called her family for breakfast just as she did every day, rain or shine. She spooned the porridge into their three bowls and they all sat down to eat.

"It's too hot!" exclaimed Baby Bear, tasting the porridge in his wee little bowl.

"We must let the porridge cool awhile," agreed Papa Bear and Mama Bear, after they tasted the porridge in their bowls.

The three bears decided to go for a walk while their hot breakfast cooled. Mama Bear took her basket in case they found ripe blackberries to put on top of their porridge.

now, it just so happened that a little girl named Goldilocks was out walking in the woods that morning, all by herself.

She had been walking since quite early, and was feeling rather tired. She was hungry as well, for she had left her house without eating breakfast. When Goldilocks saw the bears' house, she thought it was just the place to rest a bit.

Goldilocks marched right up to the front door and knocked, but there was no answer, for the bears were out for their walk. And so Goldilocks just went ahead and let herself in!

Goldilocks saw the three bowls of porridge right away, and her mouth started to water and her stomach started to rumble. She decided that she simply must taste it.

First, she dipped the spoon into the great big bowl that belonged to Papa Bear. "Oooo, this porridge is too hot!" she cried.

Next, she tried the middle-size bowl that belonged to Mama Bear. "This porridge is too cold!" she said.

Last, she had a taste from the wee little bowl that belonged to Baby Bear. "This porridge is just right!" she said, and she gobbled it all up.

After she had eaten, Goldilocks wanted to rest a bit. Looking about the room, she saw three chairs.

First, she sat down in the great big chair. "This chair is too hard!" she said.

Next, she tried the middle-size chair. "This chair is too soft!" she said, struggling to get out.

Last, she tried the wee little chair that was just big enough for her to sit in. "This chair is just right!" she smiled. But Goldilocks sat down so hard that the wee little chair broke all to pieces!

By this time, Goldilocks had grown very sleepy. She tiptoed up the stairs and found three beds there.

First, she tried the great big bed. "This bed is too high at the head!" she said.

Next, she tried the middle-size bed. "This bed is too high at the foot!" she frowned.

Last, she lay down on the wee little bed. Sure enough, she said, "This bed is just right!" And she fell fast asleep.

A short time later, the three bears returned home from their walk. They noticed right away that things were not quite right.

Papa Bear looked at his great big bowl of porridge and said in his great big voice, "Someone has been eating my porridge!"

Mama Bear looked at her middle-size bowl of porridge and said in her middle-size voice, "Someone has been eating my porridge!"

Baby Bear looked at his wee little bowl and said in his wee little voice, "Someone has been eating my porridge, AND HAS EATEN IT ALL UP!"

T he three bears then went into their sitting room. When he saw his great big chair, Papa Bear said in his great big voice, "Someone has been sitting in my chair!"

Mama Bear looked at her middle-size chair and said in her middle-size voice, "Someone has been sitting in my chair!"

Baby Bear looked at his wee little chair and cried in his wee little voice, "Someone has been sitting in my chair, AND HAS BROKEN IT ALL TO PIECES!"

he three bears tiptoed upstairs to their bedroom. Papa Bear looked at his great big bed and said in his great big voice, "Someone has been sleeping in my bed!"

Mama Bear looked at her middle-size bed and said in her middle-size voice, "Someone has been sleeping in my bed!"

Baby Bear looked at his wee little bed and cried in his wee little voice, "Someone has been sleeping in my bed, AND THERE SHE IS!"

Baby Bear's wee little voice woke Goldilocks. She sat up to find three bears staring at her—and they didn't look pleased to see her!

Quick as a wink, she rolled out of bed and ran straight to the window. She jumped right out and ran off as fast as her legs would carry her.

The three bears never saw Goldilocks again.